Tomb

of

Oaths

Dragon Riders of Osnen Book 15

RICHARD FIERCE

Dragonfire Press

Copyright © 2024 Richard Fierce

Cover design by Richard Fierce

Cover art by Nimesh Niyomal

ISBN: 978-1-958354-61-2

CONTENTS

ACKNOWLEDGEMENT

This one is dedicated to Maxwell Alexander Drake.
You helped me in a way that can't be measured.

1

The sun crested over the horizon, bathing the landscape in a warm, golden glow. I stood atop a windswept cliff and watched the countryside come into sharp focus. Squinting against the sun, I stared into the distance. Master Anesko was late. He and a small group of riders had gone out to restock our supplies, but they'd yet to return.

Something wasn't right.

They should have returned yesterday. Under normal circumstances, it wouldn't be cause for concern, but recent times were anything but ordinary now that Shadamar had declared war on the Order.

While we tried to remain within the safety of the Citadel, there were times such as now when it was unavoidable. The wind picked up, tussling my hair and pulling at my cloak.

Do you see anything?

I glanced up at Sion, who wheeled lazily overhead in a wide circle.

Nothing, she replied.

I've got a bad feeling. Perhaps we should scout around to see if we can find any sign of them.

Sion landed gracefully beside me and snorted, thin tendrils of smoke rising from her nostrils.

If Shadamar has done something to them—

You'll flame them, I said, finishing her sentence.

Indeed.

I smiled and patted her gleaming red neck scales, then climbed up her shoulder and settled into the saddle. With a powerful flap of her wings, we were airborne, climbing into the clouds. The wind stung my face, but I relished the feeling of flight. Soaring through the sky, all my problems seemed… inconsequential. Temporarily, anyway.

Sion and I moved as one, banking and diving in effortless synchrony. We twisted through a narrow ravine, timing our movements perfectly to avoid the jagged walls. I leaned into each turn, feeling the pull of momentum. Sion responded to my subtle shifts of weight, angling her wings to ride the currents rising from the valley below. Our bond was strong, deeper than words could express.

As we burst from the ravine into the open sky, I scanned the area beneath us. There was no sign of Anesko or the others. Sion's determination to find them matched my own, our twin hearts beating as one, but it wasn't safe out here. Not alone. As if to prove that, Sion sniffed the air and growled.

We've got company.

I spotted them almost immediately coming from the south. A group of five riders. They didn't need to be closer for me to know they were Shadamar's men.

We're outnumbered. Get us back to the Citadel.

Sion's rage filled the bond. She wanted to fight, but common sense prevailed and she circled back, heading for the safety of the school. The king's riders took up pursuit. Sion tucked her wings closer to her body, gaining speed as we sped across the landscape. The dragons were quick, though, and they drew closer, the shouts of their riders carried by the wind.

Hold on, Sion said.

She issued a fierce roar and flapped her wings, propelling us forward with a burst of speed. I gripped the saddle as tightly as I could, my heart hammering with adrenaline. Sion was a powerful dragon, but even she had her limits, and her haste was short-lived.

The soldiers whooped with excitement as they gained on us. I clenched my jaw and silently urged Sion to go faster. We flew past the cliffs we'd been at shortly before and the Citadel came into view. Its grand towers and thick walls towered over everything around it, a beacon of protection.

We're almost there, I said. *We can make it.*

Sion let out a defiant growl, her wings beating with renewed vigor. The riders behind us were no longer closing the gap, but we weren't gaining ground. A horn blared, and I could see people scrambling along the parapets. If the king's riders were smart, they'd give up the chase before they got too close to the walls, but they weren't letting up.

If they open the barrier, the soldiers will get through behind us.

That would be foolish of them, Sion huffed, her focus on keeping up the frenzied pace.

Yes, unless… unless they don't intend to capture us. The realization suddenly struck me. Their orders might be to kill on sight. If that were the case, then it explained why they hadn't turned back. For them, the risk was worth the possible reward.

They will not harm you. I'll flame them from existence before they get close.

The confidence behind her words brought a smile to my lips. I leaned forward in the saddle and squeezed my legs against her, knowing what she aimed to do. With a final flap, she wrapped her wings around herself and barrel rolled.

Once, twice, three times. The world spun around me, a dizzying display of color. I felt more than saw the barrier recede, and then Sion leveled out and spread her wings wide, catching the air and quickly descending to the courtyard.

I looked back to see one of the royal riders slam into the barrier. The hole that was opened for Sion was already closed, and the dragon roared in anger and pain. The others swooped up in time to avoid colliding with the magical shield, temporarily blotting out the sun as they passed overhead.

Maren rushed down from the wall, taking the stairs two at a time.

"Are you all right?"

"I'm fine," I answered as I slid down Sion's shoulder. "That was close, but I wasn't expecting trouble."

"Where are the others?"

I shook my head. "They never arrived. It's not like Anesko to be late." I lowered my voice and glanced around to ensure no one was eavesdropping. "I think they might have been captured."

Maren's expression turned grave. "We need to inform the other Curates. If Shadamar has taken them, we're in trouble. Anesko knows all the secrets of the Citadel."

"He would never reveal them," I said.

"Not willingly, no, but my uncle has used his magic to break people before. I don't doubt he'll try the same tactics now."

"I'll gather the others. We should be prepared for the worst, but we also need to plan for the inevitable. The days of mourning are almost at an end."

2

The council room was too warm. A fire burned low in the brazier, but it produced enough heat to make the space uncomfortable. I blinked several times, feeling drowsy. Almost all the other Curates had joined us, but we were waiting on Henrik.

I glanced around the table. They were all tired, their exhaustion evident by the look in their eyes. Despite that, they carried on. Would any of them bend under the weight of another problem? I hoped not. We were sorely outnumbered as it was, and although the Assembly pledged to aid us, I feared it would not be enough.

The door swung open and Henrik stepped inside. "Sorry," he grunted. "I had a few things to finish."

"No need to apologize," I said. "We're all overburdened. This will be quick."

He took a seat, and I looked at Maren. She nodded, indicating I should be the one to break the news. I cleared my throat and stood.

"As you are all aware, Master Anesko and the others have not returned. Sion and I did some scouting, but there was no sign of them. I believe they may have been captured by Shadamar."

No one moved or said anything, but the silence told me all I needed to know. Finally, Master Katori spoke.

"Have you tried to reach him by magical means?"

"I tried a few times," Maren answered. "Each time, I encountered something blocking me. My uncle is a powerful sorcerer, so it would be a simple task for him to block my magic. I'm with Eldwin on this. I think Anesko has been captured."

"This poses several problems, especially since Anesko knows things about the Citadel that no one else does." I glanced at each of the Curates in turn. "We're running low on supplies, and there are only a few days left before Shadamar marches his army back to our gates. Even if Anesko isn't being held prisoner, we need a plan."

"This is the last thing we need," Curate Mila said. She had been the one to replace Curate Josephine after her betrayal. Thinking back on that reminded me of the battle against the False King. It felt as though that had been an eternity ago.

"It is not ideal, but we've faced worse."

"Have we?" Mila huffed. "Things look pretty dire right now. I gave up my family for the Order, and now it seems that I will die for my decision."

"I, too, know what it means to sacrifice for the Order," Maren said. "It is my uncle who seeks our destruction, after all."

Mila's face flushed pink. "Yes, I know. Forgive my outburst. I'm tired."

"We all are," Maren replied soothingly. "These are difficult times at best."

I nodded in agreement. "Yes, we do not face the best odds, but I am sure we will prevail." I hoped my words sounded more confident than I felt. "Let us tackle one problem at a time. We will need supplies to outlast a siege. It will be risky, but we need to send a few groups out to get what we need. Curate Henrik, can you organize that?"

"Yes," he answered.

"Good. Whoever goes outside these walls must understand the danger, and they must return before the days of mourning are over."

Henrik nodded.

"The next issue is the barrier." The eyes of several Curates widened. I raised a hand to silence their fears. "It is secure, but we must be prepared if anything happens to it. As Maren said, Shadamar is a powerful sorcerer. I think we should shorten the shifts of those who are lending their energy to power it. If there is any weakness at all, Shadamar will find it. Master Katori, I trust you will handle that?"

"Of course."

"Thank you. We may be outnumbered, but that makes us fiercer than Shadamar's men. We have everything to lose, but they do not."

"I have an idea," Maren said. All eyes turned to her, including mine. "I know this may sound crazy, but I think we should request aid from Valgaard."

I blinked in surprise, then immediately frowned.

"We haven't heard from Valgaard since Hrodin was imprisoned for his treachery," Henrik said, speaking exactly what I was thinking. "None of our letters have been replied to."

"I'm aware of that, which is why I think we need to go there in person. I volunteer myself, since it is my idea."

"Not alone, you won't," I said. "I'm coming with you."

Katori steepled her fingers and spoke up. "We should not weaken our defenses on a whim. Who knows if the riders of Valgaard will greet you warmly or with chains? I do not think this is wise."

"It may be dangerous, but if they join us, we are stronger, and the benefits outweigh the risks."

"And if they kill you on sight, we become weaker," Katori replied.

I didn't disagree with Katori, but Maren had a point. We desperately needed help, and Valgaard was a possible answer to our dilemma.

"Master Katori outranks us all, but I think we should vote on this. I vote yes. Maren and I will go to Valgaard to seek aid. If you agree, raise your hand."

Unsurprisingly, Katori did not lift hers, but many of the Curates did.

"It is settled, then. Maren and I will leave as soon as possible. With any luck, we'll bring an army back with us. Do we need to discuss anything else?" I looked at Maren, who shook her head. None of the Curates said anything. "Very well. Let's get to it, then."

After the others were gone, I sat down and looked at Maren. "What makes you think Valgaard will help us?"

"They are prideful people. If they want to make things right, this is their opportunity. And with Hrodin out of the picture, I think it'll be easier to sway them."

"I suppose you may be right. Hopefully, no one wants to marry you this time."

Maren laughed. It had been a while since I'd heard that sound, and it brought a grin to my face.

"I'm already taken by a good man, so I would be forced to pass." Maren glanced at the door, then lowered her voice, her expression turning serious. "I've been thinking…"

"Yes?"

"Whether Valgaard agrees to help or not, there is another that could help us, but…"

"But what?"

"I don't know if things would go as planned."

"I don't understand. Who else is there?"

"Midia."

3

"Our enemy?" I stared at her, stunned.

"Osnen's enemy, but yes. There's a saying I'm sure you've heard. 'The enemy of my enemy is my friend.'"

"But… they—"

"The Necromancer and the False King did those things, Eldwin. What they did to your father was evil, but the common people of Midia did not commit those atrocities."

"Maybe not, but they allowed them to happen."

"If they did, it was because they were under duress. You know as well as I do that the False King forced his will onto them."

What she said was true, but I didn't care. The False King was one man. If the people had stood against him, they could have stopped him. I turned those thoughts aside.

"Why do you say it wouldn't go as planned?"

Maren sighed. "They are at odds with Osnen. Or rather, the leadership of Osnen. If they were given the opportunity to defeat Shadamar and end my family's line, I fear they might try to take the throne. That could plunge our lands into worse chaos than we already see now."

Her words hung heavy in the air. The thought of

seeking aid from Midia wasn't something I would have ever considered, but desperate times called for desperate measures. I supposed if there was even a slim chance that they could be convinced to join our cause against Shadamar, it was a risk we should take.

"Why didn't you mention it to the others?" I asked.

"Katori was already against going to Valgaard, and if you have uneasy feelings about Midia, imagine how everyone else will feel about it."

Images of the battle flashed in my mind's eye and I clenched my jaw, trying to weigh the consequences of what Maren was proposing.

"If we are to consider reaching out to the people of Midia, we must tread carefully. We cannot afford to let our guard down or be blinded by false promises."

"I agree," Maren said. "We will make our intentions clear, as well as the consequences should they betray us. The wounds of the past run deep, and we don't need more war in our lands. We need peace."

I nodded. "If you are set on this path, then I will trust your judgment. Midia is closer, but I think we should go to Valgaard first. If anything happens while we're gone, it'll give us the option of coming back here first before traveling into more dangerous territory."

"That was my thought as well."

Maren and I made preparations for our journey, ensuring we had enough supplies for the long flight ahead. I also made sure to grab thick coats to ward off Valgaard's freezing weather. As I saddled Sion, the weight of our mission settled heavily on my shoulders. The fate of the Order hung in the balance, and we were going to seek the aid of our enemies.

Enemies may become allies, Sion said, sensing my brooding thoughts.

I know, but our decisions are made from desperation. The choices we make could well determine the course of our future.

That is a good thing. If you can gain some control over what the future holds, it is better than leaving everything to chance.

I tightened the straps under Sion's belly and rubbed her scales affectionately. Henrik and Katori joined us in the stables to say goodbye. It was a somber parting, filled with uncertainty.

"Safe travels," Henrik said. "I expect to see you back here in a few days."

"And I expect to see this place still standing when I get back," I replied, offering as much of a grin as I could muster, considering my words.

"We will await your return," Katori said softly.

I nodded and looked to where Maren was saddling Demris. She finished with the straps and climbed up his shoulder and into the saddle. She nodded, and I urged Sion to take the lead. She leaped into the air and flew in a wide circle around the Citadel. There was no sign of the royal riders from earlier.

A section of the barrier faded, giving us our exit. Sion bolted through the hole, and Demris followed directly behind us. We turned west and flew at a quick pace. Although time was a precious commodity, there was no sense in exhausting ourselves.

Dense forests and rolling hills passed below us, and I found myself thinking about Maren's proposition regarding Midia. It seemed too risky of a move, but with Valgaard's support uncertain, we needed all the options we could get. The thought crossed my mind that Valgaard and Midia could unite against us, eliminating both the Order and the crown.

Don't be foolish, Sion said.

I know it isn't likely, but given our luck, it wouldn't surprise me.

We flew for a few hours before landing in an open field to give Sion and Demris time to rest. A stream flowed nearby, and Maren and I sat on its bank, stretching our legs. We remained silent, but her presence offered comfort that I found nowhere else except within my bond with Sion. My love for each of them was distinct, but they were equal in intensity.

"What if we get there only to find the place abandoned?" I asked. "That would explain the lack of communication from them."

"Hrodin was stubborn, as his people are. I'm sure they just refuse to respond."

"Perhaps." I wrapped my maimed arm around her and pulled her close, resting my head on her shoulder. I longed for the day that peace was restored. Maren and I had yet to talk about bringing children into this world, and while I wanted that, I knew it wasn't safe to. Not yet, anyway.

There will always be evil in this world, Sion said thoughtfully. *You must not be afraid to forge a family because of that.*

You and Maren are all the family I need right now. And what of you? Will you decide to lay an egg or two?

One day, though not anytime soon. I am still young, you know.

That's the ideal time to have children for humans. If we wait too long, it becomes impossible.

Dragons are not fragile like humans, Sion replied. She stomped over to the stream and drank of the water, then nuzzled my back, wiping her wet snout on me.

Come on. Let us see what awaits us at Valgaard.

4

I don't remember it being this cold, I complained, shivering violently against the biting wind and snow.

I do, but the cold cannot dim my flames.

Sion opened her jaws and spewed forth a torrent of fire. The warmth briefly pushed away the chill, but it returned quickly, feeling colder than before. The thick coat I brought offered little protection, but it was better than nothing. The air grew thinner the higher we flew, and Sion struggled to breathe properly.

After what felt like an eternity, Valgaard became visible as a dark blotch among the blanket of white. It sat upon the natural plateau of a mountainside that overlooked a long line of jagged peaks. It was impossible to see much of anything else because of the heavy snowfall, but Sion and Demris landed without incident.

The dragons trudged around the school to the enormous cave that was set in the mountainside, their footsteps muffled by the thick banks of snow. We stepped into the cave and the familiar network of honeycomb openings greeted us, though there were no dragons visible. I dismounted and enjoyed the warmth that radiated from the walls.

"It's been a long time s-since we've been h-here," I stuttered, glancing around as I furiously rubbed my hands together. Everything looked the same, but it was too quiet.

Do you sense any other dragons?

No, Sion replied. *The caves are deserted.*

I looked at Maren. "Sion says there are no d-dragons here. We may have come all this way f-for nothing."

"Let's check the school," she said.

Stay here with Demris. Let me know if you find anything.

I grabbed Maren's hand, and we stepped back out into the cold. The frosty air clung to my lungs, making each breath feel heavy and labored. We marched toward the entrance, our feet sinking with each step, and we left behind a trail of footprints. We reached the massive doors, their steel surface covered in a thick layer of frost. I gripped one of the handles and pulled, but the door wouldn't budge.

"Stand back," Maren said.

I moved out of the way, and she lifted her right hand, uttering a string of words. The ground rumbled briefly, and the door slowly opened to reveal a dark entryway. When we first visited Valgaard, a rider named Kell greeted us. He'd led us through this same doorway, and torches had burned brightly, lighting the way.

Now, there was only darkness.

Sion could feel my unease in the bond. *What's wrong?*

Nothing, I replied. *At least, I don't think so. We're about to go inside, but it seems empty, just like the stable.*

Perhaps they disbanded after Hrodin's treachery.

We'll find out soon enough.

Instinctively, I drew my sword and took the lead, stepping into the great hall. "Can you do something about the gloom?" I asked Maren, looking over my shoulder.

A globe of floating light burst into existence overhead, illuminating the interior of the hall. It was just as bare and cold as our last visit. I walked ahead, my eyes darting left and right, my senses on high alert.

The hall opened into a large room, and against the center wall was the throne. It was empty. A foul smell drifted on the air, and I buried my nose in my elbow.

"What is that stench?"

"Over there," Maren said.

I looked at her. She was pointing to a fireplace. Unearthly green flames flickered within it, but my attention was instantly diverted to a hunched figure sitting on the floor in front of the fire. Its back was to us, and the smell got worse as I drew closer. I used the flat of my blade to tap the figure on the shoulder, suspecting it was a corpse.

It was not.

The figure shifted and rose to its feet, towering a full foot taller than me. I brought my sword up defensively and retreated to Maren's side. A ball of flame formed between her hands, but she didn't attack the figure.

"Who is there?"

The voice sounded normal, but as the figure turned to face us, I saw the terrible truth. It appeared to be human, but its face was misshapen and looked like a strange mix between a man and an animal. I pointed the tip of my sword at the creature.

"Don't come any closer," I said.

"I mean you no harm," it replied, holding its hand up in a gesture of surrender. Its eyes, a vibrant shade of blue, held a glimmer of intelligence despite its appearance. Two horns rose from its temples, extending several inches.

"What is that thing?" I looked at Maren as if she might know the answer.

"I have no idea."

"I am no *thing*," the creature snapped. "I am a man, cursed with this appearance."

"Cursed how?" I asked.

"Tell me your names first. This is my home, and you've come in uninvited."

Before I could protest, Maren said, "I am Maren, and this is Eldwin."

"Maren Toft? And Eldwin Baines? I know your names well."

Silence ensued, and judging by the tone of its voice, I assumed the man-beast did not view us in a positive light.

"What happened here?" Maren asked. "Where are the dragons? And the riders?"

"It is a long story."

"We're a bit short on time, so make it quick," I said.

Maren cast a glare at me and turned back to the creature. "He is right. We are short on time, but I am interested in hearing your tale."

The man-beast sighed, his eyes full of sorrow and frustration. The green flames in the fireplace crackled, casting an eerie glow on the creature's twisted features.

"Long ago, when the Order first came to our lands, we fought against them and their rules. We lost the battle, and in our time of weakness, a powerful *volur* came to our aid. She convinced the Order not to slay us, and they reluctantly agreed. In return for her help, my ancestor swore an oath to her.

"He promised to live with honor despite being forced to adapt to the changing world around us. Knowing he was too prideful for his own good, the *volur* wanted to ensure he would fulfill his oath long after she was gone. She told him if his bloodline ever forsook the oath, a terrible curse would befall Valgaard. As you know, the oath was broken."

"Who broke the oath?" I asked.

"My father did," the man-beast said. "Hrodin."

5

"You're Hrodin's son?" I exclaimed.

I didn't know the former schoolmaster had a son, though it made sense he would. He viewed himself as a king, so he would want an heir to carry on his lineage.

"Yes," the man-beast replied. "I am Bryngar, the heir to the throne of Valgaard. When my father succumbed to his greed and lust for power, he broke the sacred oath that bound our bloodline to the *volur.*" He waved a hand at his appearance. "This curse is a reflection of our family's betrayal."

"I don't understand," Maren said. "How does this relate to the disappearance of your dragons and riders?"

"My father brought dishonor to our people, and they do not feel we are worthy of calling Valgaard home. They left. I am all that remains."

It was obvious Bryngar was not a threat. I sheathed my sword. "Why didn't you go with them? Why stay behind?"

"I am not worthy to be among my people."

"You didn't break the oath," Maren scoffed. "Your father did. And he is suffering his just reward in prison."

"I am not innocent," Bryngar said. "After the

Assembly took him, I tried to find him to break him free. I did not realize…" he paused and waved a clawed hand. "I did not realize the gravity of what he had done."

"Did you find him?"

"No."

"Then you technically did nothing wrong," Maren said.

"There is more. Before I understood the truth, I sent a message to our brethren far across the sea. Unlike those of us here at Valgaard, they do not have a love for dragons."

"The dragon slayers," I whispered, looking at Maren.

"Yes. I summoned them… to kill the Assembly."

"You did what?" Maren took a step forward, the ball of flame between her hands crackling with her anger.

"My father lied about why he agreed to help the dark rider Kage. I thought he was just in his intentions, but now I know better. I am sorry, though I know that does not mean much."

Maren dispelled the fire, but fury burned within her eyes. "You need to call them off. The Assembly are our allies."

"I tried, but they do not answer to me. Once they find out there are other dragons in Osnen besides the Assembly, they will bring their full might."

"They already know. They tried to kill me and Sion."

Bryngar cast his gaze to the floor. "I cannot undo what I have wrought, but I will do what I can to make amends."

"You won't be able to go anywhere looking like that," I said. "You'll be hunted like an animal."

"How can you break the curse?" Maren asked. "There must be a way."

"There is a way, but I cannot do it."

"Why not? You said you would do whatever you can to make amends."

"And I will, but I cannot do this because I am forbidden to enter the *volur's* resting place. Her magic prevents it."

Maren looked at me, and I knew what she was thinking despite her lack of words. I nodded my head slightly, so she knew I was with her.

"I must tell you why we have come here," Maren said, turning her attention back to Bryngar. "The king of Osnen, my uncle, seeks to destroy the Citadel and all who dwell there. Knowing him, he won't stop there. He'll come here next, intent upon slaughtering any rider who does not swear fealty to him. We do not have the strength to combat his armies, and we came here seeking aid. If we break your curse, will you help us?"

"Even if I didn't look the way I do now, I would

still offer my assistance. My father's actions were unjust, and the people of Valgaard will stand with you. I will need to rally them, but it will be a difficult task looking like this. If you break the curse, I will go to them. They will be relieved to know there is a way to regain their lost honor."

"How do we break the curse?" I asked.

"It will not be easy. You will need to enter the *volur's* burial chamber and place an amulet around her neck. Once that is done, the curse should lift."

I shrugged. "That sounds fairly easy to me."

"Powerful enchantments and traps guard her resting place. It is a treacherous journey, even for capable riders such as yourselves."

"Where is her tomb?" Maren asked.

"It is within the mountain. The entrance is inside the stable. I can give you a map, but I cannot tell you where the traps are. No one has been down there since she was laid to rest."

Maren nodded. "And the amulet? I trust you have it?"

"I can get it," Bryngar answered.

"Will our dragons be able to come with us?" I asked.

"I don't think so. The tunnels are said to be narrow."

Maren and I stared at one another for a moment in silence. She was a powerful sorcerer, and I had no doubts that she could disable the wards protecting the burial chamber, but we were going in blind. She stepped close to me and lowered her voice.

"We need their help."

"I know," I replied. "But we need to hurry. If Shadamar returns before we get back, there may be nothing left to come home to."

"We will do it," Maren said, turning to look at Bryngar.

"Thank you." Bryngar lowered his head in a bow. "I will get the amulet and the map. Please, eat and drink while you wait. All that is mine is at your service."

He left the room, and I waited a moment to ensure he was gone before I spoke. "Did you hear what he said? More dragon slayers will be coming."

"I heard him, but we have more pressing problems right now. One at a time, if you don't mind." She smiled and leaned in to kiss me. My lips met hers, and I wrapped my arms around her, embracing her tightly.

"You're right. Let's focus on breaking this curse."

6

After Bryngar retrieved the map and amulet, he led us out to the stable. Sion and Demris had curled up in their own caves, and Sion regarded Bryngar curiously.

He is human, but magic masks his true appearance.

Yes, he is cursed because of what Hrodin did. Maren and I are going to break the curse for him. In return, Valgaard will help us against Shadamar. You and Demris will stay behind because the tunnel is too narrow for you to fit.

Sion growled with displeasure, but when Bryngar mentioned he would feed them while we were gone, that eased her irritation.

"This way," he said.

We left the main chamber and followed him deeper into the mountain, going beyond the hatchery where I had first seen a dragon egg. Bryngar stopped at a large, circular iron door embedded in the wall. It was engraved with ancient symbols.

"Beyond this door lies the entrance to the *volur's* burial chamber," Bryngar said, his voice tinged with solemnity. "It has remained undisturbed for centuries. Be cautious and tread lightly."

"We will," Maren replied.

Bryngar pulled the door open, and Maren stepped into the gloom. Her globe of light followed, bobbing lightly as it traveled through the air. I rested my hand on the hilt of my sword and walked across the threshold, briefly wondering if Bryngar was sending us to our deaths.

"I will leave the door open for your return."

"We appreciate that," I said, his words soothing my sudden distrust. "We'll be back soon."

Maren and I walked side by side. The tunnel was long, and the shadows beyond Maren's light made it feel as though it stretched into eternity. There was a heavy silence, and the air felt stale. Faded murals on the walls depicted dragons in flight and epic battles. Maren's globe cast eerie shadows, making the scenes come to life in a ghostly dance.

Our footsteps echoed off the walls, breaking the silence and making me feel as if we were intruders treading on sacred ground.

"I can feel ancient magic emanating from… everywhere," Maren whispered. "She must have been powerful indeed."

"Do you sense any wards?"

"Yes. There is one up ahead."

I nodded and admired the paintings on the walls as we walked.

As we approached the ward, I noticed a shift in the atmosphere. The air grew charged with an otherworldly energy, crackling with power that sent a shiver down my spine. Maren pulled back on my hand.

"There it is."

Of course, I didn't see anything, but I released her hand and took a step back. She raised her hands, and the globe of light dimmed slightly as she focused her magic.

"It's an intricate web of enchantments," she said. "This is going to take me some time."

While I waited for her to break the ward, I studied one of the murals. It depicted a valiant rider atop a dragon, his sword raised triumphantly. A strange creature I'd never seen before lay on the ground, slain. I traced my finger along the lines of the picture and wondered how many stories of the past were lost in time.

I glanced back at Maren. Her brow was furrowed in concentration, and a few beads of sweat glistened on her forehead, evidence of the strain she was enduring to undo the enchantments. With a final surge of power, Maren broke the ward. I saw the air ripple faintly, and Maren's shoulders slumped.

"That was strong, even after all this time."

"You don't look so good. Do you need to rest for a moment?"

Maren inhaled a deep breath and shook her head. "I'm fine. That just took more effort than I expected."

"Take my arm," I offered, linking her arm with mine and supporting her weight as we continued ahead. She leaned on me, her exhaustion evident with every step. The tunnel seemed to stretch on endlessly. The air grew colder, and a chill settled within my bones. I shivered and pulled my cloak tighter.

Reaching a three-pronged fork, we paused and Maren looked at the map Bryngar gave us.

"Which way do we go?" I asked.

"The map only shows one tunnel in this area, so I'm not sure. Am I looking at this right?"

Maren handed the map to me. I held it out flat under the bobbing light and inspected it. Judging by the distance we had walked so far, she was right. In fact, there wasn't a three-pronged fork anywhere on the map.

"I see the same thing you do."

"Maybe Bryngar gave us the wrong map."

"Or maybe he's deceived us," I said. "He seemed too willing to help, don't you think?"

"I think he is sincere. Hrodin may have led him astray initially, but Bryngar wants to do what is right now that he knows the truth. He said no one has ever been down here before, so maybe whoever laid the sorceress to rest didn't map the way correctly on purpose."

"That's a fair guess. It's up to us to figure out which path is the right one, then." I nodded to the path on the left. "Do you sense anything down this one?"

Maren shook her head. "No. Just these two."

"Then I think it's safe to say we can skip this one. If there are no wards, there shouldn't be anything to protect."

"That was my thought as well," Maren said. "Which one should we try first?"

I studied the two remaining paths before us. The path to the right was narrower and the floor was uneven, while the one in the middle appeared wider and smoother. My instincts told me the middle path was the one we should take. I pointed to the one in the middle.

"This one seems like more effort was taken to craft it, so I think this is the correct one."

"That makes sense to me," Maren replied. "Let's see where it goes."

We ventured ahead, continuing down the main tunnel. As we walked, I couldn't shake off a sense of foreboding that settled over me like a heavy cloak. There was something about the air down here that felt different—an almost tangible presence that made the hairs on the back of my neck stand on end.

"Something isn't right," I mumbled. I drew my sword and stepped in front of Maren. The globe of light illuminated the tunnel ahead by at least a dozen paces, and there was nothing out of the ordinary in sight. I took a step forward, then another, expecting the light to reveal some ghastly creature, but there was nothing.

"Maybe I'm just imagining—" With my next step, my foot sank into the ground. A metallic sound echoed through the air, and the floor gave way beneath me.

7

For a brief moment, I was weightless.

And then my stomach churned as I fell. I stared in terrified disbelief, but before I fell too far, I stopped mid-air. Glancing up, I saw Maren's face twisted in concentration. I slowly rose until I was on the ledge beside her.

"Thanks," I said, suddenly feeling warm and sweaty. "That was close." I sheathed my blade.

"You're welcome." She smiled weakly.

"You should sit down. I know we don't have much time, but you need to rest. Your face is pale."

Maren nodded, not bothering to argue. We retreated to where the tunnel branched and sat down on the ground. Maren leaned back against the wall and closed her eyes. The glow from the orb above cast its soft aura over her, enhancing her natural beauty.

I watched her for a moment, concern gnawing at my insides. Maren was always the strong one, the one who carried us through the toughest of situations with unwavering determination. Seeing her like this, drained and fatigued, made me realize just how much it had taken for her to break those enchantments.

She had pushed herself too hard. It was my turn to be the pillar of strength, to guide us through whatever lay ahead. I turned my attention to the map again. As I studied the worn parchment, a thought occurred to me.

"What if the path without wards is the correct way ahead?"

"What do you mean?" Maren asked, her eyes still closed.

"I assumed the tunnels were protected by magic for a reason, but what if the opposite is true? What if the wards were put there to trick potential thieves into *thinking* there is something worth protecting?"

A smile crept across Maren's lips, and she cracked her eyes open. "You're brilliant sometimes, you know that?"

"I try."

We both laughed, and Maren leaned forward. She reached out and traced her finger along the lines of the map.

"If that's the case, then we've been going about this the wrong way. We need to take the path to the left. Help me up."

I stood and pulled her to her feet. "Are you feeling well enough to continue? We can leave and come back later. Bryngar left the door open for us."

"I can manage. My strength is slowly returning."

"Are you sure?"

"Yes. Come on." As if to prove her words, she strode past me. I hurried to catch up, and as we entered the tunnel, we slowed our pace. It never hurt to be cautious. After all, we could still be wrong about the traps.

"Here, let me check for more pressure plates," I said, pulling my sword back out and pushing the tip against the stones. Thankfully, none of them budged. We traversed the tunnel without incident and came around a bend that opened to another fork. Again, the map did not show the fork. Maren extended her senses, and we took the path that didn't have any wards.

Having solved the puzzle of the tunnels, we pressed on and reached the end of the labyrinth without any further obstacles. The temperature continued to drop as we journeyed deeper, and when we finally emerged from the tunnel, I understood why. Enormous chunks of glacial blue ice greeted us, forming a maze. The air was crisp, and I could see my breath as I exhaled. It was as if the very essence of winter had taken residence here. Maren's globe of light flickered, casting elongated shadows across the ice walls.

"This is incredible," Maren said, her voice filled with awe. Tiny clouds formed in front of her face as she breathed. I nodded wordlessly in agreement. The place felt almost otherworldly, as if we had stumbled upon a realm reserved for the gods. But there was no time for admiration; our task wasn't over yet. The map indicated we needed to navigate the frozen maze.

"The sorceress's body is on the other end of this," Maren said. "Magic is vibrating all around us, so watch your step and don't touch anything. I'll lead us from here."

Maren's steps were deliberate and measured, her focus on the path ahead. She seemed to have an innate understanding of this place, as if she could decipher its secrets by mere intuition. I mirrored her movements, trying to match her grace as we weaved through the intricate network of frozen corridors.

The maze seemed to stretch on endlessly. Neither of us spoke, and the silence that enveloped us felt almost palpable, broken only by the soft crunching of our boots on the icy floor. Suddenly, Maren came to a halt. I followed her gaze and saw what had caught her attention: a tomb of ice and stone covered in intricate symbols.

"That is her resting place," Maren said, breaking the silence.

I approached the tomb cautiously, my eyes scanning the intricate symbols etched into its icy surface. The surrounding air seemed to crackle with magic, and a surge of apprehension coursed through me. This was no ordinary tomb.

Maren gestured for me to stand back as she raised her hands, her fingers delicately tracing the patterns on the tomb. A soft chant escaped her lips, a melody that echoed throughout the cavern. Slowly, the ice melted away to reveal the stone beneath.

As the last vestiges of ice dissipated, a soft glow emanated from within the tomb. Maren reached out and pushed open the stone lid, revealing the skeletal remains of the sorceress. The tattered remnants of a robe covered the bones, and a metal tiara adorned her skull. It was obvious she had been laid to rest with reverence.

This woman had once wielded immense power, and now all that remained were fragile bones and a forgotten legacy. It was a reminder that no matter how much power one held; death was inevitable.

"We return this gift to you," Maren whispered. "The oath was broken, but it shall be restored."

With a somber finality, Maren carefully placed the amulet onto the sorceress's chest, right above where her heart would have once been.

"This should satisfy the curse. Can you close it back up?"

I nodded and heaved the stone lid back into place, then brushed my hands off. "Well, that wasn't too difficult."

"Not at all," Maren replied sarcastically, turning to look at me.

"If you don't count almost falling into oblivion, then this was probably the least dangerous thing we've done in a while."

The sound of sloshing water made me pause, and Maren looked beyond me. Her expression morphed from mild curiosity to dread. I swallowed hard and mouthed 'What is it?' but she wasn't paying me any attention. I grabbed the hilt of my blade and slowly turned around.

8

"Gods," I whispered in awe.

One of the ice walls had mostly melted, revealing a gigantic insect-like creature. It writhed on the ground as it struggled to get free of the remaining ice.

"She must have hidden something in her tomb to trigger the release of that thing," Maren said.

"What is it?"

"I don't know, but we should get out of here before it gets loose."

The chunk of ice cracked, and the creature was free. I stood in terror as it rose from the ground. The beast was easily ten feet long, and its segmented body had dozens of legs. It had leathery wings that were too small to use for flight, and long antennae extended from the tips of its head, each reaching several feet in length. Its icy blue chitinous exoskeleton glistened under Maren's globe of light. Sharp mandibles clicked together, emitting an eerie sound. Horns lined its back from its neck to its tail, and they glowed red with an inner fire.

Maren laid a hand on my arm, and the creature's antennae twitched, sensing our movements. Steam escaped from its fanged maw as it let out a bone-chilling roar, the sound reverberating through the cavern. It scrambled forward, leaving a trail of gouges on the stone floor. I pushed Maren behind me and brandished my sword, charging forward to meet the creature.

I slashed horizontally with my blade, aiming for the beast's underbelly. It recoiled, deflecting my assault with its armored hide. Intense pain flared up my arm, and I screamed, dropping my sword. The creature hissed a breath of scalding steam, narrowly missing me. Undeterred, it lunged, its mandibles snapping powerfully.

Magic crackled behind me, and a wave of flames rushed past, crashing into the beast. I scrambled backward on all fours, reaching Maren. She threw another blast of flames, and I watched as they swept over the creature with no effect.

"Try to freeze it!" I shouted.

Maren extended her hands, eyes narrowed in concentration, and a surge of frost burst forth, swirling around the creature. The temperature dropped even further, but the ice did nothing to injure the creature. It simply melted. Maren's brow creased with her frustration.

We needed a new plan. As the creature advanced, I racked my brain. There had to be a weakness, a vulnerability we could exploit. Maren tugged my arm, leading me around the tomb and behind an ice wall.

"My magic is useless against that thing," she huffed.

"When I struck it, my arm burned like fire." I

peeked out from the side of the wall and the creature sprinted toward our position.

"Get down!" I threw Maren to the ground, covering her with my body. The beast slammed into the wall, shattering the ice. Its momentum carried it past us, and I hurried to my feet, pulling Maren up and dragging her toward a narrow passage on the other side of the tomb. The beast turned around. Its claws scraped against the stone floor as it readied itself for another attack.

I came to an abrupt halt as the passage ended, leaving us with nowhere to go. Panic threatened to paralyze me, but I clenched my jaw and pushed the feeling aside with every ounce of strength I could summon.

"What do we do?" Maren asked.

"It's not invincible," I replied, though I found it difficult to believe my own words. "There must be some way to kill it. I don't understand why your ice didn't work. The thing was frozen."

"She must have used a spell I don't know of to trap it."

"What other spells can you use? We know fire and ice don't work."

"I know many, but I don't think magic alone is going to help us. We need to be coordinated about this."

An idea came to me. "The antennae on its head. Maybe if we damage them, it will immobilize it, at least long enough to escape."

"We can't leave that thing alive in here. What if it gets out? It would rampage through the school. No, we need to kill it."

She was right. If it could smash through a solid wall of ice, there was no telling what else it could do.

"We could crush it," I suggested. "I can draw its attention while you use magic to pin it between the ice walls."

"I like that, but I've got a better idea. I'll bring the ceiling down on it."

"You're going to destroy the cavern? I don't like the idea of disrupting the sorceress's grave. We could cause something worse than Bryngar's curse if we do."

"No, I'm not going to destroy it. I'll just collapse part of the ceiling, enough to crush the creature and seal the tomb."

"I don't have a better idea," I said. "What do you need me to do?"

"Distract it, but don't die."

The hint of a smile played at her lips, and I leaned in and gave her a quick kiss.

"If I die, I'll just haunt you as a spirit," I said with a chuckle.

"Funny. We'll need it to be near the end of the maze. I'll get into position, and you draw it toward me."

I nodded. "I'll grab my sword and lure it to the

far side of the cavern while you make a run for it. Let me know when you're ready, and I'll bring it your way."

Maren placed her right hand on my face, softly caressing my cheek while she stared into my eyes. "I love you, Eldwin."

"I love you, too."

She pressed her lips to mine, and I returned her kiss, drinking in the moment. I prayed this wasn't the end for us. Maren broke away and playfully shoved me ahead of her. Backtracking to where we entered the passage, I risked a glance into the cavern. There was no sign of the creature. I took a deep breath and silently counted, preparing myself. Nodding at Maren, I sprinted into the chamber and made a beeline for my sword.

A blur of blue color zipped overhead, dropping in front of me. The creature hissed, its mandibles snapping menacingly. I skidded to a halt, narrowly avoiding its scalding breath. It lunged at me, claws outstretched, but I sidestepped to the right and threw myself forward, tumbling to the ground beside its legs.

The beast skittered around, one of its legs grazing my left arm while another kicked my sword, sending it spinning just out of reach. Blood welled up from the shallow wound.

"Eldwin!" Maren yelled from across the chamber.

I rolled away and grabbed my sword,

scrambling to my feet. "Go!"

Maren was a blur in my periphery as she ran toward the maze of ice walls. I kept my gaze on the creature, ensuring it didn't go after her. My body tremored, both from the cold and the adrenaline pumping through my veins. I tightened my grip on the hilt of my blade, the weight of it in my hand providing a small measure of comfort.

I needed to buy Maren enough time to prepare her spell. I jabbed the tip of my sword at the creature, not intending to land a strike. It hissed again and dodged my attack, moving faster than its size should have allowed, its body lithe and fluid. I cursed under my breath, knowing I was in over my head.

A flash of light pulsed from the maze, and I took that as my sign that Maren was in place. With a silent prayer to the gods, I darted toward the maze. I navigated through its twisting paths, constantly changing direction in an attempt to confuse the creature, but its heavy footfalls grew louder behind me with every second.

I spotted Maren at the end of the maze, her hands raised. They were glowing with a pulsing azure light, casting an ethereal glow on the ice walls. I closed the distance and ran past her, turning in time to see the creature barreling straight for her. Maren unleashed her spell, sending a wave of magical energy into the ceiling.

A thunderous *crack* echoed through the cavern, and an enormous chunk of stone broke off, falling directly on top of the beast. The deafening crash echoed through the chamber and the creature was crushed beneath the stone's weight. A few smaller stones tumbled down, and then there was nothing but silence.

Time passed slowly as we waited for a sign of success. Suddenly, a bright molten substance leaked out from beneath the stone. It was hot enough to liquefy the stone and even melt some of the nearby ice.

"You did it," I said.

Maren turned to face me with a weak smile before her eyes rolled back into her head and she collapsed.

9

I rushed to her side, checking for the rhythm of her heartbeat. It was weak, but steady. I sheathed my sword and lifted her off the ground, throwing her over my shoulder. The wound on my arm throbbed, but I pushed through the discomfort and made my way through the tunnel, carefully following the map to guide me back to safety.

As promised, Bryngar had left the door open, and I returned to the caves where Sion and Demris were resting. Maren was still unconscious, and I gently laid her on the ground near Demris's cave.

What happened? Sion asked, eyeing Maren's prone form with concern.

I think she pushed herself too far. She passed out after casting her last spell.

You're bleeding. Are you all right?

I glanced down at my arm. The pain remained, but the bleeding was starting to subside. *I'm fine. Is Bryngar still here in the stable?*

No. He left after feeding us. Did you lift his curse?

We returned the amulet, so he should look normal again. Watch over Maren. I'm going to find him.

I pressed my injured arm close to my body and

left the warmth of the cave. Darkness enveloped the landscape. We'd been in the tomb longer than I thought. The wind and cold didn't seem as intense, though the trudge through the deep snow was still an arduous task. I marched to the school, suddenly heavy with exhaustion.

The door swung open easily when I pushed on it, and I slipped inside just as an unfamiliar figure was coming out of the throne room.

"Bryngar?"

"I am glad to see you have returned," he said, beaming.

As he stepped into the light, I saw that other than his size, he looked nothing like his father. His shoulders were broad and well-defined, and his muscular arms bore countless scars. Framed by a thick mane of blond hair, his face was weathered from the harsh temperatures, and his piercing blue eyes gleamed with fortitude. A bushy, reddish-blond beard reached down to the middle of his chest.

"I see the curse is broken. Returning the amulet worked just as you said."

"Yes. I felt the magic fade and looked in the mirror to see I was myself again. I am grateful for your help." He looked past me. "Where is Maren?"

"She's in the stable. The wards in the tomb drained her, and she fell unconscious after we killed a creature that was guarding the tomb."

"So it is true," Bryngar said. "The legends tell

of a guardian who watches over the *volur*. I must confess, I did not believe it was real."

"It was real," I replied, showing him the gash on my arm. "I was lucky to escape with my life."

"I am indebted to you, to both of you. I will do as I promised and rally my people. Come, let us bring Maren in here to rest. I will leave to seek my brethren, but you are welcome to stay as long as you need to."

"I appreciate your hospitality. Hopefully, Maren will wake up soon. We are pressed for time already."

We returned to the stable, and Bryngar insisted on carrying Maren.

"Do not stress your wound," he said. "It is the least I can do."

She was tiny compared to his bulk, and he cradled her in his arms as though she were an infant. We trekked back to the school, and Bryngar led us up the stairs to the second floor. The room he gave us seemed familiar, and I assumed it was the same room we stayed in the first time we visited Valgaard. He placed Maren on the enormous bed and spread a thick blanket over her to keep her warm.

"I will bring you some bandages for your arm. You can clean the wound in the bathing chamber down the hall."

"Thank you," I replied.

Bryngar left the room, and I sat on the edge of the bed and stared at Maren, watching the gentle rise and fall of her chest as she breathed. I checked her pulse again, and it was noticeably stronger than before. I was trying not to worry about her, but I was reminded of the time she fell unconscious while battling the griffon riders of Midia.

Midia.

Maren wanted to seek their aid as well. Now that we'd gained the support of Valgaard, I knew she would want to go to Midia next. That journey could be more dangerous than battling the creature in the tomb, but we needed all the help we could get. I was deep in thought when Bryngar returned, and his appearance startled me.

"You need to tend to your wound," he said firmly, eyeing me critically. "Are you feeling well?"

"I'm fine. Just thinking." I stood and accepted the bandages from him. "Thank you. As much as I don't want to spend the night here, I think it will be necessary for Maren's sake."

"I know you are in a hurry, but healing cannot be rushed, especially the kind she needs. Stay here and rest. She will not be helpful to anyone otherwise. Do you need anything before I leave?"

"You're going to travel through this weather in the dark?" I asked.

Bryngar chuckled. "I am used to it. This is my domain, after all. I will be fine. Once I have gathered my people, we will meet you at the Citadel."

"Thank you again. For everything. Other than food, I think we are fine."

"I have already prepared two packs with rations for you. You can find them on the table in the throne room."

"You are the king, yet you treat us like royalty. It is a welcome change."

Bryngar scowled. "King? I am king in name only. No," he shook his head. "I am no king, only a rider like yourself. The foolish pride of Valgaard will die. I will see to that."

I had my doubts about his intentions, but not anymore. He clapped a hand on my shoulder and grinned. "Safe travels, my friend."

"And to you, as well," I replied.

After he left, I went to the bathing chamber and washed and dressed my arm, then returned to the room and climbed into the bed next to Maren. I wanted to stay awake and watch over her, but I knew that wasn't wise. I needed my own rest. Morning would come quickly, and there was no telling what awaited us.

10

When I awoke, shafts of pale light shone through the windows. I blinked a few times and rubbed my eyes, then looked over at Maren. She was awake, her head resting against her left arm as she stared at me.

"How are you feeling?" I asked.

"Refreshed," she replied with a grin. "What about you?"

I lifted my bandaged arm and flexed the muscles, relieved to find the pain had dulled to a mere ache. "It's better."

Maren frowned. "What happened to your arm?"

"That creature from the tomb stepped on me. It left a gash, but it wasn't anything serious."

"Did we kill it? My memory is a little fuzzy."

"Yes. You brought the ceiling down on it, and there was enough blood to ensure it was dead. You passed out after that."

"And you carried me here?" she asked.

"Not quite." I relayed the details of Bryngar insisting he bring her from the stable and everything else she missed while she was unconscious.

"I wish I could have thanked him before he left. It sounds like he truly did learn from his father's mistakes."

"I'm convinced," I said. "I wasn't at first, but I am now."

Maren stretched and cuddled up close to me, nuzzling her face against my neck. "It would be nice to relax for once."

"Once this is all over, we'll make time to relax."

"Promise?"

"Of course."

"Good. I guess we should get moving. The quicker we get to Midia, the quicker we can go home."

"True." I kissed Maren on the forehead before untangling myself from her embrace. "We should eat something first. Bryngar prepared some rations for us."

Maren agreed, and together we made our way downstairs to the throne room. We sat at the table and ate a small meal from the food in the packs. A cursory glance inside them revealed bread, cheeses, some fruit, and some sort of meat. It was enough to get us to our next destination.

After we finished eating, we went to the stable and mounted up. The wind gusts weren't as fierce as the previous night, but the cold air still felt like it was freezing my bones.

We are almost gone from this place, Sion said, listening to my thoughts.

I know. Try to take us down the mountain

quickly if you can. I'm ready for the sun to warm my skin.

Sion stepped out of the cave, and I braced against the biting cold, trying vainly to shrink into my cloak. She took to the air, gaining altitude before turning east. I crouched low in the saddle and pressed my face into my arm, seeking shelter from the cold until we were out of its reach.

We flew for a few hours before landing near a densely wooded area. It was good to leave the harsh terrain of Valgaard behind. I dismounted and walked among the trees, stretching my legs. Maren joined me, and the sound of rustling leaves and the distant chirping of birds filled the air as we wandered deeper into the forest. The serenity of nature was a stark contrast to the events of the last day.

The dense canopy above created a natural shelter, and I marveled at the vibrant colors that surrounded us, from the lush greens of the trees to the delicate wildflowers that dotted the forest floor. Maren reached down and plucked a small blossom, twirling it between her fingers. Her smile was enchanting, lighting up her face like a radiant sunrise.

"Do you think I'm crazy for wanting to go to Midia?" she asked.

"Crazy? No." I shook my head. "Odd? Maybe a little." I laughed as she playfully punched me in the arm.

"I'm serious."

She sighed, her fingers releasing the delicate flower she held. It spun in circles until it landed on the ground. "It's just... I want to do what is right for Osnen and for the Order, and I know that stopping my uncle *is* the right thing, but I also fear the unknown. Valgaard was a risk, sure, but we had an idea of what we were dealing with. Not so much with Midia."

"I understand," I said. "The Order is already weak. If Shadamar falls, will the nobles squabble for power, causing more problems? We don't have the numbers to keep things from spiraling into chaos. On the other hand, what if Midia decides to invade? Neither situation would be ideal, but all we can do is hope for the best and plan for the worst."

We stood in silence, the uncertainty of the future hanging heavily over both of us.

"There's also the issue of the dragon slayers," I added. "I'm sure Bryngar will do what he can to dissuade them, but we cannot disregard the idea that we may be facing a war on two fronts while the nobles divide us from within."

You both make things sound hopeless, Sion said. *As long as you are breathing, there is hope.*

Do you not have any worries?

Dragons worry about few things, but even then, we do not let those thoughts consume us.

That's easier said than done.

You must take your thoughts captive. Bend them to your will. The future is unpredictable, but your actions today have the power to shape it. What you do today can influence what tomorrow brings.

I mentally digested her words, and they brought me a measure of comfort.

You are wiser than me, I admitted.

Of course I am. I'm a dragon. She chortled, her laughter echoing into the bond.

I shook my head, a grin on my face.

"What?" Maren asked, her expression lifting with her own smile.

"Sion. She fancies herself a comedian sometimes."

"I'm constantly fascinated by the varying personalities of dragons. Sion has a great sense of humor, while Demris is much more focused and serious."

"They are unique, just like us. I think it's easy to forget that." I paused and took her hand in mine, pulling her close. "If you think there's a chance going to Midia will help, then I say we should go. You have trusted me with every decision I have made, regardless of the outcome. I will gladly do the same for you."

Maren smiled and hugged me tightly. "It looks like we're going to Midia, then."

11

The flight to the border was uneventful. No royal riders were prowling the skies, and the wind was blowing in our favor, so we made excellent time. We crossed into Midia and as we flew over the valley where we fought the dracolich, a contingent of griffon riders swarmed up to meet us.

Sion growled menacingly, and they kept a safe distance except for the leader. He drew close and motioned for us to follow him. I nodded in acknowledgment, and he took up a position in front of us.

They led us north and Araphel came into view. Constructed on top of an extinct volcano, the castle was surrounded by an extensive network of structures that served as the headquarters for the kingdom's military. Immense catapults and ballista were carefully arranged in rows outside the protective walls. I had assumed the castle would be abandoned after the war, but it was very much still in use.

It looks the same as the day we saw it last, Sion said.

I know. It feels weird coming back here. This is where we first learned to strengthen our bond, but it's also where my father's risen corpse was enslaved.

The tangle of emotions was a complicated web.

As we landed in the courtyard, the griffon riders dispersed, leaving Maren and me alone amid soldiers bustling about their duties. Anticipation laced the air as news of our arrival spread like wildfire. Maren and I dismounted, and I glanced around uneasily, unsure if Sion and Demris would be safe among the enemy.

Do not worry about me. I will flame them all to ash before they get close enough to attack.

I patted Sion on the shoulder, and a man about my age strode over and looked us up and down. His face revealed nothing, but I had the feeling he wasn't happy with our presence.

"Since you came here peacefully, I will extend grace. What brings you to Araphel?" he asked.

I cleared my throat. "We are here as emissaries from the Citadel in Osnen. We seek an audience with your king."

The man made a noise in his throat. "Emissaries? How do I know you aren't assassins come to kill our leader?"

"You don't," Maren replied. "You'll just have to trust us. As you said, we came peacefully."

We stood in silence for a moment, and the man nodded. "Very well. Follow me."

Whispers followed us as we made our way toward the castle entrance. Inside, the familiar corridors resonated with echoes from the past. The stone walls seemed to hold the weight of countless memories, both joyous and painful. I couldn't help but feel a sense of unease creeping up my spine, a silent reminder of the battle fought within these very halls. Before he turned traitor, this was where Hrodin had killed the False King.

"Wait here," the man said, leaving us in an antechamber surrounded by armed guards. I glanced at Maren. She returned my gaze, but neither of us said anything. The minutes ticked by, and finally, the soldier returned.

"His Majesty has agreed to see you. This way."

We followed him down a long corridor, passing by portraits and tapestries that hung on the walls. The corridor ended at two thick wooden doors, which several guards pushed open as we approached.

The throne room was dimly lit. A single orb of light illuminated the center of the chamber, where a tall figure sat on the throne. Statues lined the carpet that led to the oversized chair, and spaced between them were soldiers standing at attention.

Our escort waved us ahead, and Maren and I walked side by side down the carpet. When we reached the end of the rug, we stopped and knelt in unison.

"When I received word that dragons had flown across the border, I expected to see an army at our doorstep. Instead, I see…" The king paused. "Eldwin? Is that you?"

I slowly raised my head to look at him. A face framed with a neatly trimmed white beard stared back at me. His short hair matched the color of his facial hair, and his light green eyes sparked a faint sense of familiarity. Time seemed to rewind, and my eyes widened in recognition.

"Altin?"

"You'll address the king as Your Highness," the man behind me gruffly said.

"Peace, Taran," Altin commanded. "Eldwin is a friend of mine. He is exempt from formalities." His gaze shifted to Maren. "And any friend of Eldwin is more than welcome. Rise."

Altin stepped down from the throne and came to wrap me in a hug as I stood. I returned the embrace, and he stepped back, taking in my appearance.

"I am glad to see you are still alive. How is your dragon?"

"She's good," I replied. "She is here if you want to see her."

"I would like that. Who is your friend?"

"This is my wife, Maren. Maren Toft."

Altin's brows rose in surprise as he looked at her with renewed interest. "The daughter of Erling Toft?"

"The same," Maren replied. "It is a pleasure to meet you. Eldwin told me much about his time here with you and…" she glanced at me. "And his father."

"Yes, those were troubling times. I am sad to say that I believed Dagnis's lies for too long. But those days are behind us now."

"You're the king of Midia now? I thought you fled the kingdom?" I asked.

"I did," Altin said. "Once I heard that Dagnis and his necromancer had been defeated, I came back. This place is my home, after all. I wanted to return to my shop, but the people were adamant that I take over as king. I didn't feel worthy of the title. After all I had been complicit with, I didn't think I was fit to lead anyone."

"And yet here you are."

"Here I am. The people spoke, and who am I to refuse them of what they want?"

"I am sure you are a good king," I said. "Your heart was always in the right place, even if your loyalty wasn't. The False King deceived many, not just you."

"Let us change the direction of our conversation. I do not like to dwell on the past, especially *that* part. What brings you to Midia?"

"Do you remember what you wanted from me and my dragon when we first met?"

"Yes, of course. I wanted your help."

"With what, exactly?"

"With saving my kingdom."

I nodded. "Now it is I who asks the same of you."

"What do you mean?"

"I'm not a fool of the ways of the world," Maren chimed in. "I'm sure you have spies in Osnen. Have you not heard what is happening?"

Altin shifted uncomfortably. "I've heard some rumors, but it's been difficult to distinguish the truth."

"My father decided he no longer wanted anyone to challenge his authority. He tried to destroy the Order. He's dead now, but his brother has taken the throne and seeks to finish what my father started."

"So Erling *is* dead. I heard he was assassinated."

"Not quite," I said. "He was injured, and I ended his suffering."

I expected Altin to be horrified, but he merely nodded. "Erling's ego is no surprise to me, though it is odd he wanted to destroy the Order. From what I understand, the riders have always heeded his commands. Did that change?"

"No," Maren replied. "I have my suspicions that my father was plotting something, and he was concerned that the Order would interfere with his plans."

"I see. And now your uncle wants to destroy the Order as well? That is troubling. Whatever this plot is, it cannot be good." Altin looked from Maren to me. "I am hesitant to offer my help. Crossing the border with an army would be seen as an act of war, and that would only make matters worse."

"I understand your hesitation too well, as I'm sure you remember," I said.

Altin sighed and rubbed a hand over his beard. "Indeed, I do remember," he murmured. "I cannot turn a blind eye to those in need, and I would not see another Dagnis in power, in Midia *or* Osnen. Let me consider what you've said. In the meantime, I will hold a feast in your honor. Taran, please give them lodging, then organize the preparations."

"As you wish, Your Majesty."

Altin drew close and lowered his voice. "I will do what I can to help you, but I do not yet know what that will look like. Get some rest, and I will see you both shortly."

"What about our dragons?" Maren asked.

"They will be well taken care of."

"It is good to see you again, Altin," I said.

He smiled, but there was a hint of sadness in his eyes.

12

Taran led us out of the throne room and down the myriad of corridors to an empty guest room. The furnishings were opulent compared to those at the Citadel, but there was nothing comfortable about them. While Altin was friendly and welcoming, we were among enemies. Once we were alone, I sat on a wooden bench beside the window and stared out at the battlements.

"I think we're wasting our time here," I said. "We should head back to Osnen."

"Altin said he would consider our request. Waiting is the hardest part of any endeavor."

"The look in his eyes tells me he isn't going to help us. Not in any meaningful way."

Maren joined me on the bench and stroked her fingers through my hair. "You know him better than I do. If he won't help, then so be it. At least we tried."

A few hours later, Maren and I were summoned to join the festivities. We entered the grand hall, and the sounds of music and laughter filled the air. A dozen or more tables were lined up in the shape of an enormous rectangle, and Altin was at the head of one end. He motioned for us to join him, and after we sat down, he stood and raised his goblet. A hush fell over the room.

"Tonight, we gather not only to celebrate peace,

"

but also to honor Eldwin and Maren. They are friends of mine, and therefore friends of Midia. We have overcome dark times, and now we enjoy the fruits of those labors."

The room erupted in cheers and applause as Altin raised his goblet to toast. The metallic rings of people clashing their cups together echoed throughout the room. The feast was a lavish affair, with delicacies from all corners of the kingdom laid out. Maren and I ate and drank, though I was careful not to consume too much of the mead that was being served.

A troupe of performers acted out a play that depicted the triumph over the False King. It was a humorous and lively performance, filled with exaggerated gestures and comical dialogue. The audience roared with laughter at the antics of the actors, their spirits lifted by the joyous celebration.

As I watched the play unfold, I couldn't help but notice Altin's eyes occasionally flicker toward me. There was a thoughtfulness in his gaze, and I wondered what he was considering, what decision he would make.

When the play came to an end and the performers took their final bow, Altin stood once more, holding his goblet high. The room fell silent again, anticipation hanging heavy in the air.

"I must step away for a moment, but please, continue to enjoy the food and entertainment."

Altin nodded at me, and I rose to my feet. Maren quickly wiped her mouth on a cloth, and the three of us departed, escorted by a contingent of guards. We left the great hall and went to a small chamber near the throne room.

"What's going on?" I asked, suddenly nervous. Altin's demeanor hadn't changed, but taking us to a secluded room was odd.

"Leave us," Altin told the guards. They hesitated to obey, and he waved his hands at them. "Go. I'm in no danger with them, and I will leave the door unlatched."

The guards begrudgingly exited the chamber.

"I do not want prying ears to listen to our conversation. Although I consider you my friends, there are still people in Midia who hold a grudge against Osnen because of Dagnis's lies. With time, those feelings will fade."

"Have you made a decision?" Maren asked.

"Straight to the point." Altin chuckled. His expression turned serious, and he spoke his next words slowly. "I'm sorry, but I'm afraid I cannot assist you."

His words didn't surprise me. Our kingdoms were sworn enemies, and it was a daunting request to ask someone to take on such a risk without any personal gain.

Maren's jaw tightened. "Why not?"

"My people finally have peace. That is not something I am willing to take away."

"Did you ask them if they wanted to aid us?

After all, you said yourself you don't speak for them."

"You twist my words," Altin said. "Put yourself in my position. Would you really lead your army to certain destruction?"

"Nothing is certain," I replied. "With our riders and Valgaard's, we have a formidable force. Your strength will ensure we win."

"You don't understand how dangerous Shadamar is, do you?"

"Maren is of the same bloodline. If you are worried about his magic, we have sorcerers of our own. The Citadel currently stands because of them. Magic does not give him an advantage."

"You haven't seen half of what he can do."

"And you have?" Maren asked.

"Yes."

That gave me pause. "I don't understand. You've been to Osnen?"

"No, of course not. Shadamar is cut from the same cloth as the Necromancer. Most people do not delve into dark magic by their own choice. They are drawn into it, seduced to its power by another."

"Are you saying Shadamar studied magic under the Necromancer?" I asked.

"They were both students under the same master. If I aid you, I become a target, as do my people. I do not want Midia to see any more suffering than it already has."

"So you're afraid," Maren said, crossing her arms.

"Afraid?" Altin scoffed. "No, afraid doesn't come close. I'm terrified. If you could see what I have, you would be, too. Whatever spells are protecting the Citadel can't stop Shadamar. The only reason he hasn't broken through them yet is because he's chosen not to."

A sense of dread gnawed at my insides as he spoke, and I couldn't shake the feeling that he was telling us the truth. If Shadamar was as powerful as he was sly, and I had no doubts that he was, then it would make sense he was hiding his true prowess.

"If you won't send your army, at least tell us how to defeat him."

"The only thing I know is that you cannot kill him with magic. Not unless you explore the dark arts yourself, and I do not recommend that."

Maren frowned. "Is there anything you *can* do?"

Despite no one else being present, Altin lowered his voice. "I know a group of mercenaries who will take on any job for the right price. I've hired them in the past to complete some tasks for me. They may be small in numbers, but each member is worth at least ten regular soldiers. They might just be crazy enough to go up against your uncle."

"We'll take any help we can get," I said. "But unfortunately, we don't have that kind of gold."

"Don't worry about the money. I'll take care of it."

"Thank you. I—we," I glanced at Maren, "appreciate it."

"I wish I could do more, but I can't risk it. I hope you understand."

"I don't like it, but I get it," Maren said.

"Where can we find these mercenaries?"

"You can't. I'll send them a message. If they are interested in taking the job, they'll come to the Citadel. I think they'll be apt to help you. Their leader is a former rider, after all."

13

Although it was late in the afternoon, Maren and I decided it was best to return home. We had done all we could, and now it was time to prepare for the inevitable. Sion and Demris flew side by side, and I kept a vigilant watch despite there being nothing to see. The wind whipped through my hair, carrying with it whispers of uncertainty and fear.

The impending battle loomed over me like a storm cloud. I stared at Maren for a long moment, wondering what I had done to be blessed with her. She wasn't perfect. Far from it, but she was perfect for me. She saw past my flaws, both visible and invisible, and loved me despite them.

Maren noticed I was staring and looked at me questioningly. I shook my head slightly to let her know nothing was wrong and turned my gaze ahead.

Do you think Valgaard will be enough? I asked Sion. *If Altin sent his army, I know we could defeat Shadamar. Without their help, I'm not so sure we can.*

We have seen hardships before, some more difficult than this. As long as the Order stays united, we will triumph.

Your confidence gives me hope. We flew in silence, and my thoughts turned to the mercenaries Altin had mentioned.

Do you remember when we first found each other?

How could I forget? Sion replied.

You were being taken to someone who had bought you, a mercenary leader. Her name was Seren. She was a former member of the Order until her dragon died. I wonder if Altin was talking about her group.

That seems likely. If she was a rider, I am sure she will come to help us.

Yes, I think she will. I remember she was rather imposing, but she was nice to me. She knew my father, too. None of that means she will come, though.

All we can do is wait and see.

As we reached the outskirts of the Citadel, a sense of melancholy settled over me. The familiar sights that once brought comfort now seemed tinged with sadness. The rolling hills and lush forests, which had always been a testament to our land's beauty and prosperity, now served as a stark reminder of what was at stake.

There was no sign of Shadamar or his army, and a portion of the barrier opened to allow Sion and Demris inside. We landed in the courtyard and were immediately greeted by Katori and Henrik.

"What news?" Henrik asked.

"Valgaard is coming." I didn't see the point in mentioning our trip to Midia since that had been disappointing. "Shadamar may be here by the time they arrive, but it's better they are late than to not come at all. Any luck on finding supplies?"

"Yes, and there is more good news. We found Master Anesko. He's in rough shape, but he's alive."

"Thank the gods," I said. "Where was he?"

"North of Branshire. The party was ambushed by Shadamar's men, and all but Anesko fell in battle. His dragon managed to get them somewhere safe to hide, but he's worse off than Anesko. They'll survive, but they won't be able to do much while they heal."

Our numbers continue to dwindle, I told Sion.

We will rise from the ashes stronger than before.

I wasn't so sure of that, but I kept my thoughts away from the bond.

"At least they are safe now," Maren said. "How are the preparations going?"

Henrik deferred to Katori.

"We have done all we can," she answered. "Today is the last day of mourning, and our scouts say the king's army is preparing to march. They should be here within two days. When should we expect the riders from Valgaard to arrive?"

"Hopefully before then," I replied. "The school was abandoned except for Bryngar. He was under a curse, but Maren and I helped break it, and he went to find his people after it was lifted."

Katori tilted her head to the side. "Who is Bryngar?"

"Hrodin's son."

"Can he be trusted?" Henrik asked.

"I believe so. He treated us well and seemed sincere when he told us he wanted to regain their honor. They will come. I'm sure of it."

"I hope you're right."

I could sense the doubt in Henrik's voice, but I didn't blame him. Our situation was dire, and putting our trust in those who betrayed us was a risky move, but trusting anyone these days carried its own set of risks.

Sion and Demris retreated below ground to the stables, and Maren and I went to see Anesko. He was asleep, so we left him to rest and quietly exited the infirmary. The rest of the day passed slowly, uncertainty lingering in the air like a heavy fog. As we walked through the Citadel's corridors, I couldn't help but notice the tension etched across the faces of the other riders.

After dinner, we gathered with the other Curates and discussed our battle strategy repeatedly. Each time we went through it, doubts would creep in and force me to question if we were truly prepared for what was to come.

Tired of talking in circles, Maren and I retired to our quarters, seeking solace in each other's presence. I could hear the distant sounds of soldiers marching along the parapets, the clanking of armor drifting through the window. It was a haunting symphony. Wrapped in each other's embrace, we whispered our fears into the darkness and eventually found peace in sleep.

As the days passed, anticipation hung heavy in the air. Everyone knew that defeating Shadamar would not be easy, but no one gave in to despair. The Assembly joined our discussions, offering their insights and unwavering support.

On the evening of the third day, as the sun dipped below the horizon and cast a fiery glow across the land, a messenger arrived. He carried a sealed scroll with Altin's emblem pressed into the wax—news that the mercenaries were on their way. He also delivered the news that Shadamar's forces were closing in and would soon arrive at the gates.

As the night grew deeper, I found myself restless and unable to sleep, my mind consumed with thoughts of what lay ahead. The looming battle weighed heavily on my heart, for I knew lives would be lost, and sacrifices made. But there was no turning back. We had to stand and fight because that was the only option aside from death.

A horn blared outside, jolting me awake. The first rays of dawn slanted through the window. Morning had come, and with it, the impending threat of war.

14

As Maren and I stood on the ramparts and looked out over the sprawling camp of Shadamar's army, the Citadel bustled with activity behind us. Riders scurried about, finalizing the defenses and preparing for the coming battle. Katori and Henrik, along with the other Curates, were present, overseeing the preparations.

"Any word from Valgaard?" I asked.

"Nothing yet," Maren replied.

Drums beat, and I watched the enemy lines swell, slowly gathering into orderly formations.

"What are they doing? The barrier is impenetrable. Why are they mobilizing?"

Maren's face was serious as she turned to me. "Shadamar is always scheming. The real question is, what exactly is he plotting?"

I thought about what Altin had told us about Shadamar's magic. *You haven't seen half of what he can do.* Lifting my gaze, I studied the barrier. A sense of dread washed over me.

"He's going to destroy it," I said.

"He can't."

"Can't he? How much magical energy does it take the sorcerers to keep it up?"

"A lot," Maren replied. "But they work in shifts

to keep their strength up."

"What happens when the barrier gets struck? Does it take more effort to keep it in place?"

The expression on Maren's face told me she understood what I was hinting at. "Yes, but…" She looked at Shadamar's forces. The royal riders took to the air, casting long shadows over the ground forces as they wheeled overhead.

"I think you're right, but if the barrier falls—"

"Then we need to be ready," I said. "Let's just hope that doesn't happen before Bryngar and his riders get here."

"We can't assume they'll be here in time."

"I'll warn the others."

I descended the ramparts in search of Katori and found her with Henrik. "What's the plan if the barrier falls?"

"We take to the sky and engage the enemy from above," Henrik answered. "We've already considered that possibility."

"It's not a possibility, it's going to happen. And I think Shadamar intends to bring it down quickly."

As if to prove my words, a thunderous crack split the air as ballista bolts shattered against the barrier.

"Everyone needs to be ready. Does Master Anesko know Shadamar is here?"

"Yes, he does," Katori said. "He tried to leave

his bed, but I told him to stay there and rest. He is not in any shape to fight."

I knew he probably wasn't, but if the protection of the barrier disappeared, we would need every rider we had, regardless of injuries. Saying that would sound heartless, so I kept those words to myself.

"If there's a consistent barrage, how long do we have before the shield drops?"

"Half a day," Katori answered. "Maybe longer. It is hard to say."

"That doesn't give us much time, but it's better than nothing."

We stared at one another in silence before Henrik said, "If anything happens, it's been an honor knowing you both."

Katori bowed her head.

"The only thing that's going to happen today is the death of another king." My words were heartfelt, but I knew the likelihood of us winning was almost nonexistent.

We parted ways, and I headed for the stable. Sion was in her cave. In the dim light, her eyes shone like a feline's, and her sharp claws scraped against the hard stone as she exited, her tail twitching restlessly behind her.

Is it time?

Not yet, I replied. *It won't be long, though. The battle will probably unfold in the streets.*

Sion growled, the sound sending vibrations through the stone beneath my feet. For a brief moment, I entertained the thought of fleeing. It was foolish. Where would we go? Shadamar would pursue us wherever we went. And besides that, Maren would never leave. Not willingly, anyway.

We will not run, Sion said firmly, sensing my wayward feelings through the bond. *It is time to fight for what remains.*

I know. Ignore those thoughts. They are born from fear.

There is nothing wrong with being afraid, but you must not let your fear dictate your actions. Remember what I said. You must bend your thoughts to your will.

Yes, I remember. I'll try harder.

That is all I can ask of you.

I just came down here to let you know.

We both knew I could have told her without coming to the stable, but standing in her presence gave me strength and made me feel braver than I was. She lowered her head and pressed her snout to my forehead. I rested my hands on the sides of her face and closed my eyes, basking in the moment.

As the warmth of Sion's touch enveloped me, a sense of calm washed over my troubled mind. In that simple gesture, I found solace and reassurance. Sion understood the magnitude of the task ahead, and her unwavering support only bolstered my resolve.

With newfound determination, I left the stable and made my way back to the ramparts. Maren was still there, and we stood quietly, watching as the bombardment of catapults, ballista, and magical attacks pummeled the shield. It was holding steady for now, but the strain was evident in the flickering pulses of light that emanated from its surface. The air crackled and hummed with energy, and I wasn't so sure that Katori's estimate was correct.

"We need to do something," Maren whispered.

"What can we do? We're stuck here. If we leave the Citadel, he'll follow us. This is where we make our last stand."

Maren turned to look at me. "Exactly! This is where it ends. If I know my uncle, he thinks we'll wait until the barrier falls to fight. What if we surprise him?"

"Surprise him how? We're outnumbered."

"I don't know if it's possible, but I just had an idea. We could reverse the barrier."

"What do you mean reverse it?"

"Instead of keeping it around the Citadel, we can place it over the camp. It will seal them inside."

"How does that help us?" I asked. "It'll just protect them."

"They won't be able to leave it, which effectively traps them inside. And then we can shrink it."

"If it shrinks, it'll—" My eyes widened in

realization. "You're brilliant!"

"I know." Maren smiled. "But in order to reverse it, we'll have to drop it first. That will leave a brief window of time where we aren't protected."

"It's worth the risk. And if we fall, we will fall together."

15

While Maren aided the sorcerers with the new plan, I was in the courtyard with the other riders, mounted and ready for anything unexpected. I absent-mindedly rubbed Sion's neck scales while my eyes remained on the barrier.

Projectiles relentlessly pummeled the barrier, targeting a specific portion. We evacuated everyone from the area behind that focal point, anticipating significant destruction once the barrier faded.

On top of the ballista bolts and magical attacks, the royal riders occasionally flew overhead, their dragons breathing their flames onto the shield. It flickered with every strike. At first, I thought it was a sign of its impending failure, but it became evident it was merely a visible display of the strain on those keeping it up.

We should be prepared to fight the king's men if the barrier falls while they fly overhead, Sion said.

Maren said they will drop the barrier when there's a lull.

I felt Sion's muscles tense under me. *I can feel the magic receding. Get ready!*

The seconds ticked by and there was no change. Slowly, sections of the barrier rippled and became wispy like dye poured into water before dissipating from view. Several ballista bolts flew over the walls and crashed into the ground. A moment later, a bolt of lightning zig-zagged across the sky and struck the western side of the Citadel, scattering broken pieces of stone.

A cheer rang out.

They think they destroyed the shield, I said.

We could use that to our advantage. Come on!

Sion leaped into the air. I gripped the reins tightly as she ascended, her powerful wings beating against the air.

What are you doing?

Drawing their attention, she replied. *If they focus on us, they won't breach the Citadel.*

A chorus of roars filled the air as the other riders took to the sky behind us. We soared over the wall, the wind whipping through my hair. Below us, chaos ensued. Thinking they had broken through the barrier, Shadamar's men charged forward without hesitation. There were so many of them. They streamed across the land like a tidal wave, their armor flashing under the morning sun.

Sion unleashed a fiery breath that engulfed a group of soldiers pushing a battering ram toward the main gates. They screamed, and I scrunched my nose in disgust as the stench of burning flesh hit my nostrils. An arrow whizzed through the air near my head, and Sion banked sharply to the left, smashing her tail into the center of a siege tower. The wood splintered and men cried out as the upper portion fell, crushing them as it collapsed to the ground.

We darted over the battlefield, Sion's fire and claws tearing through the enemy ranks. The other riders followed our lead, descending like a storm and ravaging everything in their path. Chaos settled over the battlefield as the soldiers, realizing the ruse, began scrambling to retreat.

I admired the ferocity of our attack, and the element of surprise had given us an advantage, allowing us to strike fear into their hearts, but I knew it wouldn't last. We were outnumbered, and the royal riders were circling to engage us.

Get back to the Citadel, I said. *The tides are about to turn against us.*

Sion ignored me, her lust for battle in control. The bond flooded with her rage, and she breathed a long torrent of flames, sweeping her head left and right. The cries of the wounded and dying drifted up to us. Instead of trying to push through her fury, I scanned the battlefield looking for Shadamar.

A horn blared, and I glanced over my shoulder. Behind the school, an immense mass of clouds quickly approached.

What is that? I asked, but Sion was deaf to my question.

It grew closer, and I smiled as soon as I realized it wasn't clouds. It was an army of white dragons. Bryngar had rallied his people. Valgaard had come!

My fist shot up as I let out a battle cry. Sion joined me, matching my roar, and the white dragons echoed our cries with a deafening boom that seemed to shake the very air.

We can do this, I thought. *We can end this here and now.*

Yes, we can, Sion growled, reading my mind. *There's the king!*

I turned my attention ahead and saw him. He rode a black horse, and a contingent of mounted soldiers in plate armor surrounded him.

Why isn't the barrier up yet? It's taking too long. Something must be wrong.

I can sense something. It's subtle, but I think it's blocking the spell from forming.

It's coming from Shadamar, isn't it?

There was a pause before she answered. *Yes.*

Take me to him.

I could feel Sion's hesitation in the bond. *He won't let us get that close.*

She was probably right, but I knew that wasn't why she said it. She feared for my safety. I did, too. If he were an ordinary man, I would have no issue defeating him in fair combat, but Shadamar was anything but ordinary.

Take me, I repeated.

Sion rumbled her objection, but she veered toward his position. As we got closer, the battle intensified. The white dragons clashed with the royal riders, their roars and screeches filling the air. Flames and ice swirled above our heads, casting a ghostly glow onto the battlefield. Sion propelled us forward with incredible speed, dodging arrows and spears.

She dove, her massive wings tucked in as we descended. The ground rushed up to meet us, and I braced myself for impact. Sion's talons touched down, raking furrows into the dirt, and I leaped off her back and drew my sword in one fluid motion. Sion towered behind me, snapping her jaws menacingly.

"Surrender," I shouted. "Surrender or die!"

<h1 style="text-align:center">16</h1>

"You've brought friends," Shadamar said with a sneer. "It won't matter. The Order will die today."

He dismounted from his horse and ordered his guards to stand aside. A surge of adrenaline coursed through my veins. This was it—my chance to end this war. Sion let out a thunderous roar that echoed across the battlefield. I lifted my sword and took a defensive stance, but I knew Shadamar was unlikely to give me a fair fight.

Tell me if you sense he's using magic, I told Sion. *I can't defend against it, but maybe I can draw his focus enough that Maren and the others can get the barrier back up.*

I will.

"Why do you want to destroy the Order? It's been around for centuries and has always aided the crown."

"Aided the crown?" Shadamar laughed. "That means nothing to me. The Order has grown weak. It is a hindrance to progress, and without new dragons, the Order will die off. Better to end it quickly now than to watch it suffer and fade slowly. Your dragons are nothing more than glorified pets."

I am no pet, Sion growled.

Shadamar wagged a finger at her. "Don't do anything foolish."

"You're lucky she hasn't flamed you yet," I said.

"Let her try. Her flames cannot harm me."

Don't humor him. Let's just keep him busy.

"You bore me. I don't understand what my niece sees in you. You're crippled, a low born, and have nothing to offer her. Like the rest of the Order, you are a leach on society."

I'd heard worse insults growing up as a child. "If you surrender now, we'll let you live out the rest of your days in the dungeon. Otherwise, I'm afraid you won't be leaving here alive."

"Don't play with me, boy. I could snuff the life from you with a snap of my fingers."

"Fight me like a man," I taunted. "No magic. Just steel and skill."

Without warning, Shadamar lunged forward, his movements swift and calculated. His sword flashed from its scabbard faster than I thought possible, but I managed to parry his first strike, our blades clashing with a resounding clang that reverberated through the air.

Sion's protective instincts kicked in, and she sprang past me, her maw coming within inches of Shadamar's head before she came to a sudden stop.

"No dragons, either," Shadamar said. He flicked his wrist and Sion was thrown aside by an invisible force. She tried to get up, but something kept her pinned down.

"Don't touch her," I said through clenched teeth.

"I'm only leveling the field."

I attacked, and Shadamar parried my thrusts effortlessly. His movements were graceful and fluid, leaving me struggling to keep up. We continued to exchange blows, the clang of each one ringing loudly in my ears. Sion remained pinned to the ground, but her presence was an unwavering source of strength.

He's toying with me, I told Sion. *He's faster and stronger than I am.*

It's subtle, but he's enhancing his movements with magic.

I wish I could do the same.

Pull what you need from the bond to keep your strength up. I can feel the exhaustion rising in you.

I drew on Sion's strength and immediately felt my energy return. Breaking away from Shadamar, I wiped the sweat from my brow. "You're using magic. I thought maybe you had more honor than Erling, but obviously not."

My words must have struck a nerve because Shadamar's face twisted in anger, and he snarled. The air hummed, causing the hairs on my arms to stand on end. Tendrils of black shadows flew out from him and struck me, sending me reeling backward. I crashed into Sion's immobile body, but quickly regained my footing. The tendrils retreated and faded from view.

What was that?

It was dark magic, Sion replied. *You should flee.*

I'm not leaving you here. We still need to draw his focus away from blocking the barrier spell.

He will kill you. You need to run.

Shadamar's guards looked up and began shouting. He ignored them, and they turned their mounts around and spurred them into a gallop. I glanced at the sky and saw the reason for their hasty retreat. A white dragon had been killed and his body was falling straight toward our position.

With no hesitation, Shadamar uttered a few words and conjured a cone of vibrant red energy from his right hand. The powerful beam shot through the sky with incredible speed before colliding with the fallen dragon, sending it careening off course. With a deafening crash, the creature tumbled to the ground a short distance away, creating a cloud of dust and scattering clumps of grass in its wake.

I looked at Shadamar and wondered why I thought I could defeat him.

You are stubborn, Sion said. *And you don't listen to me.*

Sometimes I do.

Not when it matters. Run. Please.

I looked Sion in the eyes and slowly shook my head. "I'm tired of running." Turning back to face Shadamar, I tightened my grip on the hilt of my blade. Every second I kept his attention was another opportunity for Maren and the other sorcerers to get the barrier back up.

"Let's finish this," I spat, lunging forward. We clashed in a flurry of blows, but Shadamar was as agile as a feline, dodging every one of my strikes with ease. It was as though he could guess what I was going to do before I did it.

He's reading your body language, Sion said. *Don't be so obvious about what you're going to do.*

I considered her words. He had more battle experience and was using his magic to augment himself, but that didn't mean he couldn't be defeated. Something Katori once said to me suddenly echoed in my mind: *Amidst chaos, there is always a chance for success.*

Shadamar was reading my movements, but what if I could trick him? I feigned left and went right, dodging his sword and thrusting my blade at his leg. The tip of my sword struck him and cut a gash in his thigh, surprising both of us.

In the blink of an eye, his hold on Sion slipped and she scrambled up, swiping at him with her claws. He backpedaled, cursing as blood soaked his pant leg. I pressed my advantage, hacking and slashing wildly. With every step he took, blood spurted from his wound. He roared in pain as he parried my strikes, but before I could land another hit, he unleashed a torrent of dark energy, engulfing me in shadows.

My vision blurred, and I stumbled backward,

swinging my blade to ward off an attack. None came. When the darkness cleared, Shadamar was gone.

17

Where did he go?

Sion's tail flicked behind her as she gazed around the battlefield. *There.* She bounded away, leaving battered soldiers in her wake. I sprinted after her, the ground trembling beneath my feet as she ran.

We need to catch him before he escapes, she said. *The barrier is forming.*

I glanced back and saw the air rippling with magic. I pushed my legs harder, holding my sword behind me. Sion leaped into the air, gliding over the wreckage of a toppled war machine. I went around it, dodging enemies to keep up with Sion.

She spun about, crashing her tail into a swarm of soldiers. They went flying in every direction, and she pounced on Shadamar, pinning him to the ground with her claws. Magic flared from him, and Sion screeched in pain, but she didn't release him. I slowed to a jog as I got closer and jabbed the tip of my sword against Shadamar's throat.

"You've lost," I huffed, out of breath. "Surrender."

"You think that if you kill me you win?" He laughed, madness in his eyes. "I am nothing compared to what's coming."

I stared at him, unsure what he meant.

"Do it," he snarled. "Kill me. Kill me like you killed my brother!"

My nerve faltered, and I looked at Sion. She kept her focus on Shadamar.

Let's go, I told her. *The barrier will take care of him.*

He deserves to die.

And he will. He has caused suffering using his magic, and now magic will end his life.

I removed my sword from his neck. Sion didn't move. I could feel her hatred burning through the bond.

You said yourself we need to hurry. The barrier is expanding.

The air hummed as magic flowed into the barrier. The battle raged on, and no one paid any heed to the impending doom.

As soon as I let go, he will use his dark magic against us.

I had the same thought, but maybe we can take flight before he gets a spell off.

Remove his tongue, Sion said.

He can still cast spells with hand gestures. I've seen him do it.

Then cut off his hands, too.

I hesitated, knowing it was a ruthless tactic, but the urgency of the situation made me consider it. We had to survive, and I knew Shadamar would stop at nothing to kill us. I knelt and grabbed Shadamar's right arm, pulling it free from under Sion's claw.

"You're just a pawn in someone else's game," he hissed.

"Maybe, but pawns can still win." I brought my sword down as hard as I could, severing his hand from his arm.

Surprisingly, Shadamar didn't cry out. He forced his eyes shut and his body tremored, but no sound escaped his lips. It was a gruesome act, and I despised doing it, but it had to be done. Moving to the other side, I cut his other hand off. Blood gushed from his wounds unabated, drenching the ground around him.

Now his tongue, Sion demanded.

The thought of doing that made me queasy. *I can't. This is enough. Come on, let's get out of here.*

Shadamar's body went limp, and his head lolled to the side.

He's no threat to anyone unconscious, I said.

Satisfied, Sion lifted her claw. Shadamar remained where he was, lifeless except for his erratic breathing and the rise and fall of his chest. I wiped my sword off and sheathed it, then climbed up Sion's shoulder and into the saddle. She took to the air.

"To the Citadel!" I shouted as we flew over the battlefield. "Riders, return to the Citadel!"

Whether they ignored me or just couldn't hear over the din of battle, nobody retreated. The Valgaardians had routed the royal riders, and the army below was in disarray. I felt lightheaded as magic teased my mind, and Anesko's voice echoed in my thoughts.

Flee the battlefield while you can. The barrier will seal anything in its path. Stay at your own peril!

The vertigo faded, and I held on to the saddle as Sion swooped around and sped across the sky to get beyond the barrier's reach. Once we were out of harm's way, she slowed her pace and we watched as the barrier closed over the battlefield, enveloping most of the enemy's forces.

The barrier was a sight to behold—a shimmering wall of energy that was as tall as it was wide. I couldn't fathom the amount of magic that powered the spell. It remained in place for a moment before slowly shrinking. It consumed everything it touched, leaving the ground scorched and ruined.

Screams erupted as the barrier burned people alive, turning them to ash. Sion and I watched grimly as the magic ravaged the battlefield, silencing the cries for help and leaving nothing but glowing embers and dust behind. Even the trebuchets and ballista were scorched from existence.

The aftermath of the barrier's destruction was horrifying. Sion and I hovered over the swath of destruction, unable to turn away from the scene. As we flew over the now desolate battlefield, I vainly searched for Shadamar's remains, but there was nothing left. An entire army had been erased in mere moments. Sion offered comfort through the bond as emotions overwhelmed me.

What have we done?

We did what was necessary.

We had no choice. That's what I told myself, over and over. The cost was high, but the loss of life was necessary.

I hope this never happens again, I said.

No one knows what the future holds, but I do not foresee things going this way a second time. This will serve as a warning to our enemies. The arena of war is a playground for sorcerers.

As we flew back to the Citadel, I couldn't help but wonder how many innocent people had been caught in the crossfire. Despite everything Shadamar had done, I couldn't shake the feeling that we were no better than the monsters we fought against. We had survived, and the balance of power had shifted in our favor. What we did with that power would reveal if we truly were monsters.

I prayed we weren't.

18

As the days turned to weeks, the battle felt more like a dream than a reality, but the charred field in front of the Citadel was a constant reminder that it had truly happened. The mercenaries that Altin had sent arrived after the battle was over. It turned out their leader was Seren Gray, the mercenary I'd met back in Tiradale. She had been Geoff's employer, the man I'd worked for when I first found Sion.

Just as Altin had assumed, she was eager to help. Her former days as a rider may have been long gone, but her sense of loyalty remained. She and her band set out to track down the soldiers who'd escaped the battle. Their fate was in her hands now, and I suspected she would not be very forgiving.

I sighed and closed the book I was reading, setting it on top of the growing pile to my right. Now that one problem had been solved, it was time to deal with the next one. Bryngar had said that the dragon slayers were from a land beyond the sea. So far, I had yet to find anything useful about where it might be located. I stood and stretched, rubbing my lower back where an ache throbbed from sitting too long.

"Bryngar said he sent a message to them, yet he doesn't know where they are," I said, looking at Maren. She was sitting at the desk across from mine, also flipping through books for clues.

"Yes. I asked him about that. He said he used some sort of spherical item to send the message. I'm certain it's magical in nature, but that doesn't help us. You don't need to know where someone is physically to communicate with them, but it is limited by distance. Somehow, this item isn't affected by that. It takes extreme focus and a lot of energy to send a message from here to Valgaard. I can't imagine the amount of magic it would take to send something across the sea."

"I haven't found anything that indicates there are lands anywhere beyond the sea, but that doesn't mean anything. I mean, we found that old royal outpost when we sailed to find the wild dragons, so I'm sure there are other lands out there."

"We already know there are," Maren said. "Remember when we saw the elven and dwarven souls on the ferry?"

My eyes widened. "I forgot all about that! You're right. Now that I think about it, there was an elf who said dragons were servants in his land. Do you remember that?"

"I do. We aren't trying to find elves or dwarves, though. The dragon slayers were humans."

"True."

I walked to one of the tall windows and stared out at the courtyard below. The sun was setting, bathing the sky in hues of orange and scarlet. The western side of the school had suffered significant damage during the battle, and rubble still littered the area around it. Anesko said the repairs were going to take a few months. His injuries healed well, and he was back to normal.

"If the dragon slayers bring an army with them, we'll have to leave the Citadel behind," I said. "We don't have the strength or the numbers to fight another war."

"The Order can be rebuilt," Maren replied. "And Bryngar said he will do whatever he can to stop them from coming here. We have to trust things will work out."

"Yes, but we should plan for what happens if they do not."

Silence fell between us, and I turned to face her.

"When does this end? When do we get to make a life for ourselves instead of worrying about everyone else?"

"What are you talking about, Eldwin? This *is* our life. We're riders. It is our duty to live selflessly."

I rubbed my face. She was right. It was my exhaustion speaking. "Sorry," I muttered. "I should probably get some rest."

"I'll come with you," Maren replied, closing her book and standing.

She grabbed my hand, and we walked the empty halls together back to our room. My life had gone down a very different path than I ever expected, but I couldn't complain. I had found Sion on this path— and Maren—and I knew deep down that we had to continue on this journey. There was no room for selfish desires.

Despite the constant dangers and challenges we faced, we had done it together. We had saved countless lives, and there was no doubt our sacrifices had made a difference. Whatever tomorrow brought, we would face it together, side by side, as riders.

As family.

THE END

ABOUT THE AUTHOR

Richard Fierce is a fantasy and space opera author. He's been writing since childhood, but began publishing in 2007. Since then, he's written multiple novels and short stories.

In 2000, Richard won Poet of the Year for his poem *The Darkness*. He's also one of the creative brains behind the Allatoona Book Festival, a literary event in Acworth, Georgia.

A recovering retail worker, he now works in the tech industry when he's not busy writing.

He's married and has three step-daughters (pray for him), three dogs (two huskies!), three cats, two ferrets and a fish. He basically has a zoo.

His love affair with fantasy was born in high school when a friend's mother gave him a copy of *Dragons of Spring Dawning* by Margaret Weis and Tracy Hickman.